Tales of the RAF / **BOOK TWO**

Fighter Escort

D0034857

A Hindsight™ Collectible

BOOK TWO

"FIGHTER ESCORT"

Captain Dawson and the rest of the Royal Air Force 14th Squadron escort a formation of American bombers flying into enemy territory. The RAF pilots are responsible for protecting the Americans on their way to the target, and bringing them home safely. This dangerous mission will test the bravery of everyone involved. Meanwhile, twelve year old Harry Winslow "falls" into a dilemma of his own. Unsure of what to do, Harry discovers a confidant in the colorful American, Captain Sam Ross, pilot of the Texas Buckaroo.

Join Harry on the airfield when the 14th Squadron's thundering fighter planes fly "Fighter Escort" for their American allies. See how these men risk their lives to protect their country, friends, family, and their fellow fliers. These are the ordinary people who do extraordinary things. The kinds of things that make them heroes.

Fighter Escort

By DON PATTERSON
Illustrated by Sonny Schug

Hindsight Limited, PO Box 46406, Eden Prairie, MN 55344.

ISBN 1-929031-09-2
Library of Congress 99-096395
Copyright ©1999 by Hindsight Limited. All rights reserved.
Printed in the U.S.A.
First Hindsight™ printing, October 1999

PICTURE CREDITS
Many thanks to the following organizations for giving permission to reprint illustrations and text used in the "In Hindsight" section of this book:
pp. 90-91- Time Life Books, The Air War in Europe, Alexandria, VA (Courtesy of United States Air Force)

Written by Don Patterson
Illustrated by Sonny Schug/Studio West
Edited by Mary Parenteau
Production by Kline/Phoenix Advertising Graphics

To Ron, Mary and Sonny.

The pilot gets the credit,
but really it's the crew
who's responsible for success.

TABLE OF CONTENTS

"FIGHTER ESCORT"

CHAPTER ONE

A NEW DAY

Shafts of sunlight filtered through the early morning fog hanging over the fields of Hampton County, signaling the start of a new day. Roosters crowed in the distance, awakening the surrounding countryside. However, the ground crews at Hampton Airfield had already started their day several hours earlier preparing the 14th Squadron's Hawker Hurricanes for flight.

Striding through the thinning gray mist, Squadron Leader, Captain Ted Dawson, stopped to watch the busy mechanics on the hardstand. Briefly scanning the activity, Dawson faithfully knew the ground crews would have his squadron of twelve fighter planes ready for the next mission. Satisfied with their work, he continued on his way to the Operations Building for the seven o'clock mission briefing.

As usual, Captain Dawson was early, and the

first to enter the briefing room. The briefing room was the largest office in the building. It was furnished with twelve leather chairs, arranged in rows of three. They faced an old oak desk. Here, Dawson and his pilots would soon be told about their mission.

Taking his familiar seat, Dawson stretched his legs and glanced out one of the small windows overlooking the airfield. He restlessly waited for the other pilots to assemble. Peering through the dirty glass, he focused on the ground crews preparing the Hurricanes lined up along the

hardstand. Dawson noticed the men refueling the planes were taking extra precautions to double check the fuel tanks. Already a seasoned veteran at only twenty-seven years old, he knew that when so much effort was applied to refueling, the upcoming mission would be a long one.

Dawson's attention quickly shifted away from the airfield when Captain Simms entered the room.

"Ted," Simms started abruptly, "you should've

been at breakfast this morning. There was quite a scene!"

Captain Dawson thought to himself for a moment, and with a wry smile asked, "What did Gainey do to Hyatt now?"

Amazed at Dawson's perceptive response, Simms shook his head. "How did you know it was about them?"

"It's always those two, Andy," Dawson replied. "So tell me, just what did our most mischievous pilot do now?"

Simms, who was second in command of the squadron, sat down in the worn chair next to Dawson and proceeded to tell him the story.

"Apparently, Lieutenant Gainey submitted a rather colorful mission report. As I understand it, he took credit for fifteen enemy fighters destroyed in only one mission. Then he recommended himself for an immediate promotion to Air Vice Marshall!"

Dawson chuckled at the thought of the outrageous report. "I see," he mumbled. "All right, Andy, then what happened?"

Simms blurted out, "He signed the blasted

thing with Hyatt's name!" Leaning over in his chair he continued, "Colonel Harrison got a hold of the report and didn't find it funny at all. While we were eating breakfast, the Colonel marched in and exploded at Hyatt for wasting his time with such an 'idiotic' story. Then he canceled Hyatt's weekend leave as punishment. Once the Colonel left, Hyatt jumped across the table and went right after Gainey's throat."

Now Dawson understood the harm in Gainey's practical joke on Hyatt. Shaking his head, he said "Those two fight like..."

"Cats and dogs," Simms finished.

"No," Dawson corrected, "worse yet, they fight like brothers. They continually brawl with each other. But, when one of them gets in trouble, the other will do anything to help him out."

After a short silence Dawson remarked, "I suppose I need to straighten things out with the Colonel so Hyatt can get his leave back."

"Not this time, Ted." Simms explained in a fatherly tone. "It's Gainey's responsibility. I told him to fix things with Colonel Harrison by the start of our mission briefing, or I would fix him!"

Dawson agreed with Simms, and the two

men continued to chat while the rest of the pilots
began to gather in the room.

Eventually, Captain Dawson's concentration
returned to the activity outside the window.
Glancing across the field, something caught his
attention on the far side of the hardstand. A faint
smile stretched across his lips when he recognized
the head of thick brown hair, and slight frame of
Harry Winslow. Harry was watching the mechanics while sitting in his usual spot on the small hill
just behind the hedgerow that ran along the airstrip.

Hampton Airfield bordered the Winslow farm. For years, the open land had been used to graze sheep. When the German army swept across Europe in late 1939, Britain prepared to defend itself and constructed a network of Royal Air Force airfields throughout England. Soon to become one of the new RAF airfields, engineers quickly built hangers and leveled the empty field next to the Winslow farm in order to make an airstrip.

About the same time, Harry's father, at the request of the Prime Minister, joined the Intelligence Service and left to work in London. Since then, the airfield had become a fixture in the landscape. And in the absence of his father, the squadron of pilots had become increasingly important to twelve year old Harry Winslow.

A frequent visitor to the small air base, Harry and the men of the squadron have become quite close. Possibly even too close, considering the dangerous occupation of the fighter pilots. Perhaps for just that reason, Harry spends as much time as he can with his adopted RAF family.

CHAPTER TWO

MISSION SPECIFICS

At exactly o'seven hundred hours, the base commander, Colonel Harrison, entered the briefing room. All twelve pilots of the 14th Squadron rose to attention and watched him stride to the oak desk in front of them.

Harrison quickly turned around to face the restless group. With a salute, he matter-of-factly greeted the men.

"At ease, gentlemen, and good morning."

The pilots returned to their seats while Colonel Harrison arranged some papers on the desk top in preparation for the briefing. Once again, Captain Dawson's thoughts drifted back to the airfield, and the crews refueling the fighter planes. Thinking of missions that would stretch the range of their Hurricanes, a list quickly ran through his head...coastal patrol, continued alert status, or...

Dawson's daydreaming abruptly ended when he heard Colonel Harrison announce, "Fighter escort for a bombing mission is today's draw."

Harrison pointed to a large map hanging on the wall and began to discuss the details of their mission. "A formation of American bombers is

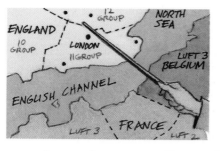

flying across the Channel to the French coast around Calais." Tapping at the map with a pointer, he explained, "You will meet them at the rally point, here, just past Dover."

Then Harrison turned away from the faded map and stepped back to the desk. Leaning over the polished top, he continued the briefing.

"Gentlemen, you will be escorting a group of forty-eight B-24s to their target and back. Their mission is to knock out the supply lines that feed German coastal airfields and fortifications. Now watch out for those Yanks, some of them may lose their bearings and get lost flying around up there. Show them just how valuable a Royal Air Force escort can be."

"Remember, men," Harrison warned, "we are not flying today to simply run up the tally of downed enemy fighters. We're responsible for protecting those bombers. Your mission is to bring those lads home safely."

Colonel Harrison stopped and glared at Lieutenant Gainey, "That includes you, Gainey, or should I say, 'Air Vice Marshall'? If we lose one bomber while you're chasing...how many was that? Oh yes, fifteen Me 109s, you'll be packing parachutes until the war is over!"

Boisterous laughter from the other pilots echoed off the walls. Embarrassed, Gainey flushed beet red and shrank down in his chair. His bright crimson face stood out in stark contrast to his fair skin and blonde hair. Undoubtedly, Gainey had fixed the problem between Hyatt and the Colonel, but it was clear he would suffer teasing from the rest of the squadron for days to come.

Harrison paused for a moment. Returning to a serious tone, he asked the pilots, "Are there any questions?"

Dawson and his men remained quiet. Their mission was clear.

"Then, that is all, gentlemen." Looking at his watch, Harrison informed the anxious group of aviators, "To make the intercept point, you'll need to be airborne in less than thirty minutes. Take to your planes."

The Colonel grabbed his notes, signaling the end of the briefing. The men in the room rose to attention. In response, Colonel Harrison saluted the fighter pilots and watched them leave.

Noticing Captain Dawson nearing the door,  Harrison called out, "Ted, mind your fuel gauge today."

Dawson stopped and replied, "Yes sir, I'll fill a juice can with petrol and bring it with me, just in case."

The two men smiled knowingly at each other, and then Dawson left for the airfield. Colonel Harrison could hear the deafening roar of fighter plane engines warming up outside while he stood alone in the room.

Walking together, the close knit group of RAF pilots made their way to the awaiting planes. After passing on some last minute instructions to his men, Captain Dawson climbed into the cockpit of his fighter. Captain Simms followed and quickly jumped into his own Hawker Hurricane. While tightening the straps to his seat, Dawson's eyes swept past the line of Hurricanes on the hardstand and focused on the small grassy hill where he had noticed Harry earlier.

Still there, Harry was now standing at attention, his right hand held stiffly above his eyebrows. Dawson returned a crisp salute to his young friend, and then flashed a thumbs up sign. Happy to have simply been noticed, a broad smile washed over Harry's face.

Amid the rumbling engines, the ground crews shouted instructions and gave the pilots hand signals to prepare them for take off. Dawson then motioned to Simms that it was time to go.

The two veteran pilots raced their fighters across the rugged field and lifted skyward. One by one, the rest of the 14th Squadron's Hawker Hurricanes followed, bouncing along the grassy runway and climbing into the air. After the very last plane scrambled to join the squadron, Hampton

Field grew quiet once again.

Harry watched the assembling RAF formation bank toward the southeast. As they turned, a quick flash of morning sunlight reflected off the glass canopies. When the planes leveled out, he lost sight of them against the bright blue sky.

CHAPTER THREE

THE NEW KITE

Once the thunder of the Hurricanes' engines faded into the distance, Harry heard someone calling to him.

"Harry!" a small voice rang out over the field. "Grab your kite and let's go!"

Harry looked up the dirt path leading back to his house. There was Stuart with his younger sister Erin. Excitedly waving their arms,  they continued shouting for his attention.

Harry had known Stuart since before he could remember. The two boys were the same age and close companions. Two years younger than her brother, ten year old Erin was friends with Harry in her own right. Although Stuart and Harry had much in common, Erin was the one who shared Harry's passion for the pilots and planes of Hampton Airfield. Often the two would sit together for hours on the small hill overlooking the hardstand, watching the men and their fighter planes.

With the 14th Squadron away, Harry was happy to see his friends, and even more excited for a chance to try out the new kite he had made.

Running up the well-worn path, he called out, "I'll get my kite and be back in a second!"

Too impatient to wait for Harry, Stuart began unwinding the ball of string connected to his kite. Worn from use, Stuart's kite was little more than tattered gray paper loosely stretched across a spindly wooden frame. Gracing the front was a hand drawn picture of an eagle. Erin helped Stuart with a few tangled knots and then carefully held the faded kite while her brother unwound some more string.

With the screen door slamming shut behind him, Harry ran out of the house and leaped from the porch racing to join Stuart and Erin.

"I just finished it last night!" Harry announced.

Proudly, he presented his new kite for Stuart and Erin to inspect. They closely examined it. Stuart eyed the crisp seams that ran around the edge, tightly

holding the wooden cross pieces together. Erin
was impressed by the bright white paper and tail
made from blue-gray cloth tied to the point.

"Well," Harry asked, seeking their approval,
"tell me, what do you think?"

Stuart looked at Erin and the two children
nodded their heads.

"She's a beauty," Erin said in awe.

"That's for sure, Harry," Stuart agreed, "but
will she fly as high as mine?"

"There's only one way to find out," Harry
replied. "Let's put them up in the air!"

The excitement of a friendly challenge
charged through the boys. Erin held onto the two
kites while Harry and Stuart each paced away
with leaders of string. When a stiff breeze swept
across the yard, Erin tossed both kites high into
the air. At that moment, Stuart and Harry took
off running. Catching the wind, the kites soared
up into a bright blue sky.

When the boys finally neared the hedgerow
fence at the end of the field, Harry and Stuart
stopped and turned to face their kites. Erin joined
them and all three watched the dancing kites
sweep from side to side through the air. Pulling

tightly, the friends wrestled with their strings trying to make the kites fly higher.

"Harry," Stuart said breathlessly, "she's..."

"Glorious," Erin finished.

Proud of his kite, but considerate of his friends, Harry replied, "Thanks, Erin. Wouldn't you say she flies almost as well as Stuart's?"

Stuart smiled at Harry's unselfish comment. "Aren't you going to paint a picture on it?" he asked.

Harry scratched his head, and answered, "I want a picture that looks like one of Captain Dawson's planes, but I'm not that good at drawing a Hawker Hurricane."

"Could your sister do it?" Erin asked.

"Nah," Harry replied, "all she can draw is a bunch of flowers. I don't know anyone who can draw a good fighter plane."

"We'll find someone, Harry," Stuart assured his friend. "And it will be great when it's done."

The laughter and happy conversation of the three children carried on, echoing across the meadow while their kites flew high in the sky over Hampton County. For the moment, the destructive war raging throughout the world around them was far away.

CHAPTER FOUR

THE TEXAS BUCKAROO

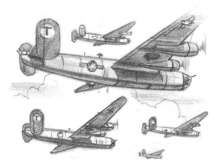

The thundering roar of forty-eight American B-24 Liberators assembling overhead rattled windows throughout the city of Dover. The huge four-engine, twin-tail bombers had become a common sight during wartime.

Although allied bomber formations often flew over the area, enemy bombers also passed overhead on their way to English targets. This time, the bombers were flying east out over the English Channel.

The people of Dover, going about their morning business, smiled in relief when they recognized the large American star painted on the underside of the huge wings of each airplane. Both young and old, gazing upward, reassured each other of their safety for the time being. Still, it was only after the last plane flew over the roof tops and out to sea, that life returned to normal on the city streets below.

Meanwhile, Captain Dawson was leading his squadron on a southeast heading to join the American bomber formation at the rally point. Within fifteen minutes of leaving Hampton Airfield, the swift RAF fighter planes were approaching Dover. The white cliffs along the coast sparkled in the bright morning sun. While surveying the scene below, Dawson's headset crackled with a message from one of his men.

"Captain, I see our big brothers straight ahead!"

Returning his attention to the horizon in front of him, Dawson confirmed the large American formation.

"They're pretty hard to miss, aren't they?" he replied.

Closing in on the slower moving American planes, Dawson adjusted his course and speed to bring the squadron alongside the Liberators. Escorting a group this large, he thought about repositioning his planes to cover both sides of the formation. By splitting into two smaller groups of six Hurricanes each, one led by Dawson and the other by Captain Simms, they could more readily protect the Americans from enemy fighters.

"Andy," Captain Dawson radioed to Simms, "let's split the squadron here. I'll stay and cover the left side."

"Roger, Ted," agreed Simms. "I'll cover the right from above."

Simms signaled to the pilots in his group and started to climb. Five other Hurricanes broke from the squadron and followed Simms up and over to the other side of the formation. Just as Simms and his men settled in above the right side of the bomber group, a distinctive voice rang through Captain Dawson's headset.

"Howdy, boys! Captain Sam Ross here, United States Army Air Force! Y'all must be the ones takin' us to the dance today!"

Dawson quietly chuckled to himself as he listened to the American's heavy southern accent fill the radio.

"Good morning to you, too," Dawson replied. "Captain Ted Dawson and the rest of the RAF

14th Squadron at your service."

Again, the radio boomed with the voice of the American flyer. "Our mission must be really important to git you RAF boys up here so early in the mornin'."

Dawson called back, "Fighter Command is worried you chaps won't be able to find your way home without us."

Captain Ross, the pilot of the lead B-24, and commander of the mission, called to his navigator in the nose of the plane. "These Brit fighter jocks seem to think you ain't gonna be able to drive us home after the party. Whatch y'all think of that?"

The navigator acknowledged the teasing with barely a nod and a shrug of his shoulders. Captain Ross slapped his leg and let out a hardy laugh.

Then he radioed back to Dawson, "We'all been here once or twice before and gotten home all right. But its nice havin' some 'Little Friends' just the same."

A bit curious, Captain Dawson examined the lead American plane. He noticed two things. First, painted just behind the glass nose of the B-24 was a picture of a cowboy on a bucking horse.

"...the quiet ride they were enjoying would soon come to an abrupt end"

The name "Texas Buckaroo" was inscribed below it. Second, Dawson counted thirty-five small bombs, as well as twelve enemy planes and one ship, painted just under the pilot's window. The title "Texas Buckaroo" explained the American's accent. And the thirty-five bombs, representing thirty-five missions, said a lot about the veteran pilot and crew.

Surveying the eastern horizon in front of him, Captain Dawson watched the French coast gradually roll into view. Beyond the sandy beaches he could see clouds rising over the green mainland casting dark shadows on the distant ground below.

Each man in the formation knew that the quiet ride they were enjoying would soon come to an abrupt end. There wasn't a chance that the sound of sixty airplanes thundering through the skies over occupied France would go unnoticed. Most likely, the discovery of the American bombers and their RAF escort would result in a launch of enemy fighter planes, flown by German pilots determined to cut them down.

CHAPTER FIVE

FIGHTERS CLOSING

 Anticipating an attack, it was no surprise to Captain Dawson when he spotted a squadron of sleek German Messerschmitt 109 fighters closing in on his position. Dawson radioed a warning to the entire formation.

"Everyone, heads up! Bandits closing at ten o'clock!"

Before the message was even finished, the allied pilots and crews prepared for the unavoidable battle to come.

Dawson quickly called to Captain Simms, "Andy, stay with the bombers. We'll fly to intercept."

"Roger," Simms hastily responded.

Dawson and his squad broke away from the

formation to engage the oncoming German fighters. In an attempt to out maneuver the English planes, the squadron of Me 109s split up. However, the six RAF pilots immediately responded to the enemy's strategy. Captain Dawson and three more Hurricanes banked hard left to pursue one group of Me 109s, while the other two fighters looped to intercept the remaining German planes.

Instantly, the battle reached full force. White-hot tracer bullets blazed dotted lines through the sky when the opposing planes opened fire at each other. Flying in wide circles, the English fighters skillfully worked to contain the German squadron, holding them back from the eastward moving bomber formation. As a measure of their success, Dawson watched the B-24s pass safely into the distance.

While Dawson's half of the squadron held the deadly enemy fighters at bay, Captain Simms continued to escort the American bombers to the mission's target. Ahead, the rising clouds had thickened.

Passing over the French coastline, Simms spied the fortifications the Germans were building into the beaches below. Concrete bunkers bristling

with field guns and other artillery dotted the once peaceful, sandy bluffs. Continuing inland, they had less than fifteen miles left to reach the target area. But Simms knew these would be the toughest miles of the mission.

"Men," Captain Simms radioed to the formation, "there's no way we're going all the way to the target without more action, so be..." A blast of machine gun fire hurling past his cockpit cut the message short.

"B-Flight, break with me!" Simms shouted through the radio and rolled his plane into a steep banking turn. The squad of Hawker Hurricanes followed Simms away from the Liberators to battle the new wave of Messerschmitt fighters pouncing on them from behind the gray cloud cover.

Preoccupied with his dangerous situation, Simms barely noticed the American commander's voice ringing through his headset.

"I'm takin' the boys down through the clouds to three thousand feet so we can get a clean look at the targets."

"Roger," Simms quickly responded. "We'll hold the fighters, then catch up to you!"

Concerned for the English pilots, Captain Ross cautioned his new friends, "You RAF boys take care now, ya' hear."

Simms noticed the bombers gently angle earthward while the battle with the Me 109s raged. The small RAF group soon found themselves overwhelmed by the attacking Germans. Caught in the whirlwind of combat, the headsets of Simms and his pilots sparked with messages from each other as they struggled with the cunning enemy fighter planes.

"Hyatt, watch your left, two Bandits closing!" crackled in the pilot's headset.

"See 'em!" Hyatt responded, and quickly veered to avoid the incoming fighters.

"Three more diving from above!" Captain Simms urgently informed his men when he spotted several more German planes joining the battle.

"I flamed one!" Gainey called into his radio.

The rest of the pilots looked around to see flames and thick black smoke pouring from the Me 109 Lieutenant Gainey had crippled.

"Brian, one down all right, but watch the other one on your tail!" warned Lieutenant Hyatt, while flying above and behind Gainey's plane.

Listening to the message, Gainey twisted in his seat to look back. The risky situation became all too clear to the young pilot when he saw sparks flicker from the firing guns of the Messerschmitt bearing down on his Hurricane.

"Break right, Brian, break right!" Hyatt shouted into his radio as he closed in behind the menace that was stalking Gainey.

At Hyatt's direction, Gainey rolled his plane sharp right, and out of Hyatt's way. The moment Gainey's Hurricane cleared the line of fire, Hyatt triggered his weapons. He could feel his plane suddenly shake when all eight machine guns poured into the German fighter in front of him. The Me 109, that moments before threatened Hyatt's friend, lurched into a steep dive. A twisting trail of smoke traced its path to the ground.

Gainey radioed to Hyatt, "Thanks for the help, James. I really owe you one this time!"

"You did manage to get my leave back," Hyatt replied, "so we're even...for now!"

Just then the familiar voice of Captain Dawson filled the radio, "Could you lads use a little help?"

Struggling to hide his relief, Captain Simms sarcastically called back to Dawson, "Feel free to join us if you have the time. But I must tell you, it's a little hot right now."

The sound of Dawson's and Simms' customary chatter sparking across the radio immediately lifted the spirit of every pilot in the squadron. Finished with the first wave of fighters, Dawson and his men raced to join Simms and his pilots fighting the second group of enemy planes. Reunited, the full squadron of British Hurricanes could overpower the German fighters.

Dawson adjusted his goggles and then ordered into the radio, "Mix it up gentlemen!"

"The remaining German planes...turned from the fight..."

Once Dawson's group joined the battle, the tone of their radio messages changed from caution to calculation. The hunted had become the hunters. Soon, three more Me 109s were pushed out of the deadly game, spiraling earthward in flames. The remaining German planes, hopelessly outnumbered, turned from the fight and raced away to safety. The only enemy pilots left in the area were the ones slowly drifting to the ground in parachutes.

CHAPTER SIX

THE TARGET

Thanks to their RAF fighter escort, the American bombers had reached the target area unscathed. With the Texas Buckaroo leading the way, the B-24 Liberators descended below the gathering clouds and prepared for the bomb run.

"Two miles out boys, so get ready!" Captain Ross, radioed to the entire group. "And y'all keep your heads up for ground fire."

The formation spread out when the bombardiers began to spot the specific roads, bridges, and railway lines used to supply the German build-up at the coast. Just as Captain Ross had warned, the crews in the B-24s could see enemy ground forces firing at them when the thundering formation neared a set of bridges connecting to a railway yard.

"You call it, bombardier!" Ross radioed to the anxious lieutenant sitting in the nose of the plane.

Hunched over his bombsight in the Texas Buckaroo, the bombardier took control of the

plane's heading. Peering down
to the ground below, he skillfully
maneuvered the B-24 to drop
the bombs on the fast approaching
target. While the bombardier
kept a steady approach to the

arched steel bridge, other Liberators headed for
the railway yard less than a mile to the north.

Pressing the release trigger with his thumb
at the precise moment, the bombardier called to
the crew, "Bombs away!"

Seconds later, bright flashes and plumes of
black smoke rose from the ground. Five more
B-24s following the Texas Buckaroo also dropped
their payloads on the bridge. From his position in
the back of the Buckaroo, the tail gunner watched
the trestle give way and collapse into the river it
used to span. In similar fashion, the railway yard
to the north of their position burst into flames
after being hammered by other bombers in the
group.

"Where's that oil depot, boys?" Captain Ross
barked over the radio. "We ain't done 'til we hit
that oil depot!"

The gathering clouds had thickened over

Calais and the entire French mainland. A shifting wind pushed the planes from side to side. Soon, poor weather would force any aircraft out of the area.

Flying dangerously low because of the cloud cover, Captain Ross was all too aware of the worsening situation. The formation of B-24s raced to their last target before either the storm or more German fighters could stop them.

"Time to finish the mission, boys!" Ross radioed to the group. "Y'all with bombs left, find that oil depot! The rest of us are gonna soften the place up a little with some machine gun..."

"Chief, I see six, no seven, bandits at nine o'clock low!" the Texas Buckaroo's waist gunner shouted.

"There's five more coming up at twelve o'clock!" the co-pilot warned.

Seconds later, the American bomber formation was under attack by a swarm of German fighters. The protective guns in the B-24s sparked to life as the crews took aim at a fresh squadron of Me 109s fearlessly screaming through the flock of American planes. Caught between buffeting winds and the speedy attack of the German Messerschmitts, the cluster of Liberators was breaking up and spreading apart.

After making several passes over the bombers, the German fighters regrouped and concentrated their attack on the B-24s flying straight for the final target. The oil depot, by far the most important target of the mission, was only a mile away.

From the corner of his eye, Captain Ross noticed the bomber flying to his left, the "Sledge Hammer", was blanketed by enemy planes. Hopelessly out gunned, one of the four engines burst into flames and the B-24 began to lose altitude. Spewing a wide trail of black smoke, the battered American plane slipped below the flight path of the rest of the formation.

Suddenly, the Texas Buckaroo was rocked by a rain of bullets from the German squadron's machine guns. The Buckaroo's gunners fiercely returned fire on the attacking Me 109s, but to no avail. Enemy fire ripped through the plane's skin and smashed into instruments, cutting electrical and hydraulic lines. Thick gray smoke began to

fill the cabin of the damaged bomber.

"Chief, engines one and two are on fire!" the co-pilot frantically yelled through the smoke.

Captain Ross reached forward to his instrument panel and called out, "Cut power to one and two!"

The American fliers quickly flipped a series of switches to stop the fuel supply that fed the burning engines.

"Fire suppression and feather the props," Captain Ross continued, using a calm, seasoned voice.

The co-pilot flipped more switches and confirmed his Captain's orders.

"Roger Chief!"

Ross and his co-pilot watched their burning engines. Finally the yellow flames flickered out. Luckily, the immediate danger from the engine fire was over.

For the moment, the weary crew of the crippled Texas Buckaroo was relieved to see the vicious German fighters break away from their plane. But their concern resurfaced as they helplessly watched the Me 109s focus their attack on other bombers further back in the formation.

Just then, the huge round storage tanks of the oil depot came into view. Captain Ross stiffened in his seat, determined to attain his goal.

Although the German fighter planes had rattled the Americans, they hadn't stopped them from reaching the final target. The tail gunner in the Texas Buckaroo watched strings of bombs release from several other B-24s and plummet to the ground. A high pitched whistle pierced the air as the staggered rows of bombs fell toward the earth.

When the explosive payloads crashed into their target, the tanks ruptured, and oil burst into flames. The Texas Buckaroo shook from the blast. Looking back over his shoulder, Captain Ross could see thick black smoke rising into the air from fuel burning out of control.

Turning forward, a smile brightened Captain Ross' grimy face. The moment of satisfaction from a successful mission, however, was all too brief. The battered Liberators were still in enemy territory, still fighting German Me 109s, and still a long way from home.

CHAPTER SEVEN

THE SHIFTING WIND

Harry and his friends, Stuart and Erin, ran through the fields keeping their kites aloft, even in the shifting wind. They had worked their way back across the Winslow yard and were nearing a wooden fence bordering the Reid farm.

Dark stories about Mr. Reid had made him well known to the children in Hampton County. Rumor had it that Mr. Reid hated everything, except his chickens. Practically everyone used the nickname "Mad Man" Reid when telling tales about the haggard old man and his rundown farm.

While their kites continued to soar high in the sky, Harry and Stuart pulled at the taut strings causing them to sway in the air.

"Hey, you two," Erin warned. "Your kites are getting awfully close to each other up there."

"Stuart keeps crowding me," Harry defiantly complained.

"Just keeping you on your toes, Harry," Stuart teased. Then he tugged at the string to steer his kite even closer to Harry's.

The combination of Stuart's good natured play and a sudden shift in the wind caused his kite to twist and dart across the sky. The kites collided, and their strings hopelessly tangled together. Stuart and Harry feverishly jerked at their lines trying to free the two tumbling kites.

Watching the situation unfold, Erin announced in an alarmed voice, "They're falling..."

A frustrated Stuart shouted back, "We already know that, Erin!"

Erin continued, "They're falling onto 'Mad Man' Reid's chicken coop!"

Harry and Stuart looked up from the hastily wound wads of string just in time to catch a glimpse of the kites crashing onto the roof of Mr. Reid's weathered old shed. In a desperate attempt to pull the kites free of the splintered wooden roof, Stuart yanked at his line. With a snap, a limp coil of string sprang back from the tangled kites and wrapped around his hand. The lines broken, Harry and Stuart had lost touch with their kites. For a long moment, the three youngsters silently eyed each

other, unsure of what to do next.

Stuart fell back into the grass and in a defeated tone said, "Well, it was a beat up old kite anyway."

"Mine's not!" Harry shot back. "It's brand new. We've got to go and get it!"

Stuart simply shook his head, refusing to make any attempt to help. If retrieving his kite meant having to go on the forbidden property and disturb old man Reid, Stuart would rather it be lost forever.

"Harry," Erin explained, "we can't! If 'Mad Man' Reid catches us, we'll be in big trouble! Forget about it! Let's go do something else."

Determined to get the kites back, Harry said nothing. Undaunted, he hopped the fence and started for the old shed. As he marched across the field, he could hear clucking from the startled chickens. Fearful the hens might make even more noise, Harry cautiously approached the rundown chicken coop.

As luck would have it, some old crates were lying next to the small shed, offering Harry a way to climb onto the rickety roof. He piled the crates one on top of the other. Then, steadying himself against the side of the shack, he stepped on top of the wobbly pile and carefully pulled himself up to the roof.

Happy to see the wayward kites, Harry quickly reached across the rotten wood shingles. Just as he was about to grab them, he heard the flimsy peak beneath him make a creaking sound. At that instant, the shed gave way, collapsing to the ground under Harry's weight.

Feathers spewed into the air! An explosion of terrified chickens scattered in all directions from the splintered wreck of the coop. Stunned, Harry stood up in the middle of the mess, and gazed at his friends.

Back across the field, Stuart and Erin looked in amazement at the calamity. Then, they frantically started jumping up and down and urgently began pointing at something. Standing in a rain of feathers, rubbing his bruised arm, Harry turned to look in the direction they were pointing. He panicked at the sight of old Mr. Reid hurrying toward him and the demolished shed.

Still dazed, Harry looked back to his friends

for support.   But their small frames were already shrinking into the distance as they bolted away across the field.

Not knowing what to do, Harry scrambled from the broken bits of shed and scattering chickens. He ran after his disappearing companions, but they were already out of sight. Never stopping to look back, Harry could hear the angry voice of Mr. Reid calling out.

Sprinting away from the disaster, Harry anxiously searched his mind for a solution.

"Surely old man Reid saw us," he thought.

"He'll tell Mother and I'll spend the next ten weeks in my room!"

Frightened and confused, Harry ran to the one place where he felt safe. He quickly scurried to the gap in the hedgerow fence that opened onto Hampton Airfield. Concealed from all around him, hopefully, there, he would figure out what to do.

CHAPTER EIGHT

THREE ALONE

Their mission complete, Captain Ross radioed to the entire formation of B-24s. "All right, boys, we got the job done. Let's head back to the barn! Climb to fifteen thousand feet, into the clouds for cover, and head due west."

At Captain Ross' command, the bombers began their ascent to the relative safety of the storm clouds gathering overhead.

Noticing the rest of the formation slowly climbing away from them, the co-pilot of the Texas Buckaroo looked over at Captain Ross and said in a quiet voice, "Chief, we can't keep up with only two engines. We'll be sitting ducks for those Me 109s."

Captain Ross looked knowingly at the co-pilot, and then keyed his radio to speak to the rest of his crew.

"Men," he announced, "facts is facts. With only two engines, we're falling behind the other boys. Once the rest of the formation has made it to the cloud cover, we're gonna stick out like a sore thumb. So watch for those fighters when they come, and let's take a couple of 'em down with us!"

After a brief moment of silence, the rest of the crew called back to the captain of their damaged plane, "Roger, Chief, we're with ya."

Captain Ross watched the last of the B-24s in the formation disappear into the clouds above, leaving the swarming Me 109s to take their revenge on the remaining Americans. Peering through the cracked glass windows of his cockpit, he noticed that two other badly damaged Liberators were struggling to stay in the air along with the Texas Buckaroo. Ross felt relieved to know the plane he saw attacked earlier, the "Sledge Hammer", was still flying. The third plane, the "Tall Order", slowly caught up to the other war-weary bombers.

Ross radioed the crews and ordered them to tighten up their three-plane formation on his lead. While the damaged B-24s turned west for home, the German fighters regrouped and began to dive at the abandoned bombers.

"While the damaged B-24s turned west for home, the German fighters regrouped..."

"Here they come, mad as bulls!" Captain Ross radioed to everyone in the three remaining planes.

The waist and top turret gunners in the B-24s began defending their ships from the eight Messerschmitts screaming toward them. The roaring guns of the German fighters ripped through the crippled Liberators. In return, a hail of bullets from the Americans hurled through the sky in a bold attempt to stop the Me 109s from coming closer. Spent shells piled up on the floor of the Texas Buckaroo until the last round was fired. Then the guns fell silent, and the American crew bravely prepared for the worst.

Suddenly, the diving enemy fighters broke from their pattern, scattering in all directions.

Amazed by the erratic behavior of the German planes, Captain Ross questioned his co-pilot, "What's goin' on up there?"

No sooner had he asked, than his question was answered. The American's "Little Friends" had returned. Sweeping past the three lumbering bombers, a group of RAF Hawker Hurricanes trained their guns on the Germans.

Captain Dawson, leading five other RAF fighters, engaged the Messerschmitts at speeds

up to two hundred miles per hour faster than the damaged bombers could fly. The crews in the battered American planes watched the brave English fighter pilots rally against the enemy. White trails of vapor traced lines through the sky as the fighters tangled with each other.

The men in the bombers cheered when one of Dawson's pilots triggered his guns on an incoming Me 109 and sent it spiraling in an uncontrollable dive. Moments later, a second German fighter fell victim to the brutal dogfight. Low on ammunition, the last German planes turned east in defeat, clearing the once dangerous sky.

Starved for fuel, Dawson and his pilots were relieved to see the end of the battle and immediately veered west. Following the trail of black smoke, the Hurricanes quickly rejoined the damaged B-24s struggling to reach the safety of the English Channel. Having saved the bombers from disaster in France, Dawson and his men reformed to surround the American planes and escort them home.

CHAPTER NINE

A SHAKY RIDE HOME

"Well, Captain Ross," Dawson radioed to the American pilot. "It looks as if we will take the low road home today."

Dawson referred to the fact that the crippled American planes were in no condition to climb above the storm clouds.

"Gettin' home is all that counts. It don't really matter how," Ross replied with some relief in his voice.

Then he asked, "Say, where are the rest of my boys?"

Dawson radioed back, "Simms and his lads are watching over them up above the cloud cover. They must be about twenty miles ahead of us by now."

Pleased to know the rest of the bomber formation was in good hands, Captain Ross looked out his shattered window at the French coast line

passing below. The entire crew breathed a sigh of
relief when they headed out over water, back to
England, and home.

For the first time since
coming under fire, Ross took
a moment to inspect his cockpit
and instruments. On the panel
in front of him there seemed to
be more bullet holes than gauges.
Broken bits of glass were everywhere, and frayed
lengths of electrical wire dangled from the walls
and ceiling of his plane. Fortunately, no one was
injured. Miraculously, his plane was still capable
of flying.

Captain Ross called to the other two bombers
in order to check on the amount of damage they
had sustained. When the others radioed back,
describing their situation, it was clear that the
sooner all three planes were on the ground, the
better.

"Captain," Ross called to Dawson, "me and
my boys here ain't gonna make it all the way back
home to our base at Manchester."

"Roger," Dawson replied. "Why don't you
spend the night with us at Hampton? Our

mechanics will fix your planes and you'll be on your jolly way in a day or two."

Ross looked at his co-pilot. Both men, fully aware of their condition, agreed that the RAF base was the best option. The Americans would have preferred to make it to their home base at Manchester. But Hampton was closer. Setting down there would significantly reduce their dangerous flying time.

The American pilot keyed his radio, and with his thickest accent told Dawson, "Now that's down right friendly of you, Captain! I'll radio my other crews and tell them we're gonna follow you home to Hampton Field."

While Captain Ross informed the other two B-24 pilots of the plan to set down at Hampton, the coast of England came into view. The men in their faltering planes cheered when they saw the rocky beach pass under their wings.

Upon reaching the safety of English soil, Captain Dawson ordered four of the six RAF fighters to speed ahead to Hampton. Dawson and Lieutenant Mathews, flying the only two Hurricanes with enough fuel left, remained to escort the three struggling Liberators the last miles to their landing field. Smoke continued to trail from the battle-damaged bombers as they approached the small RAF fighter base that would be their temporary home.

CHAPTER TEN

FINAL APPROACH

"Prepare for final approach, boys," Captain Ross radioed his men. "And look tight for the crowd."

Ross' co-pilot laughed to himself. Shaking his head in disbelief, he flipped switches and checked the few remaining operational gauges in preparation for landing.

"Whatch y'all laughin' at?" Ross asked the co-pilot.

"Well, Chief," he replied, "how do you look tight with a plane that has lost two engines, is barely able to fly, and..." The co-pilot suddenly stopped in mid-sentence.

Ross glared at him and asked, "And what... what else?"

Looking worried, the co-pilot finished, "And has no landing gear."

Captain Ross shifted in his seat and mumbled under his breath, "If our luck changes, we might just git outta this alive."

Ross radioed his situation to Captain Dawson. Trying to help, Dawson dropped his Hurricane several feet in order to inspect the underside of the Texas Buckaroo. The English fighter pilot saw the twisted metal and broken hydraulics that prevented the Buckaroo's landing gear from lowering.

Dawson drew his plane back up alongside the damaged B-24 and called to Ross, "Captain, I'm sorry to inform you that your undercarriage is a bloody mess!"

"Thank you for that 'comforting' description of my landin' gear!" Captain Ross sarcastically replied.

"All right," Ross continued, "there's nothin'
we can do about it up here. I think it's time you
and yer wingman went home. Then the other two
Liberators can put down. I'll bring the 'Buckaroo'
in last for the big finish."

"Roger, Captain," Dawson said with some
hesitation. "For what it's worth, old chap, welcome
to Hampton, and...good luck."

"Thanks for the help, Dawson. You and yer
boys ain't bad considerin' you're Brit fighter jocks!"

Then, Dawson and Mathews, the last of the
fighter escort for this mission, rolled their planes
and broke from the three bombers. Circling to
the northeast, the fighter planes straightened out
and made a direct approach to land at Hampton
Airfield. Throttling back on the engines, the last
two Hurricanes descended to the landing field and
touched down. As the planes slowed, their tail
wheels dropped into the grass.

On the ground, Dawson and Mathews taxied
their exhausted fighters to the hardstand. His
part of the mission over, Captain Dawson rolled
back the canopy of his plane, climbed out of the
cockpit and hopped to the ground.

Out of habit, Dawson glanced over at the

Winslow hedge. As usual, Harry was there, although this time he was impatiently pacing about. Captain Dawson signaled for Harry to come and join him on the hardstand. Dashing through the small opening in the bushy fence, Harry ran across the field to meet him.

"Captain Dawson!" Harry called. "I need your help with something."

Dawson bent down to speak to Harry, "Just a minute lad, those Americans up there are in trouble."

Absorbed with his own problem, Harry hadn't noticed the sputtering B-24s circling overhead. When he sensed Dawson's concern for the safety of the Americans hovering above, his troubles began to shrink in comparison.

"Harry," Captain Dawson explained, "those men have had a tough time of it. Mathews and I were the only ones with enough fuel to hang back and escort them home. For all they've been through already, it looks like landing could be the most dangerous part of their mission."

Harry could hear the worry in Dawson's voice. Then he asked, "What can we do?"

After a long moment watching the

American planes struggle, Dawson finally looked at Harry.

"Harry," Dawson started in a resigned tone, "I'm afraid there's nothing we can do now. It's all up to them."

CHAPTER ELEVEN

BARELY ABLE TO LAND

Simms and the other RAF pilots joined Captain Dawson and Harry out on the hardstand to watch the Americans. The engines of the three war-weary Liberators thundered and popped overhead as they prepared to land at Hampton Field. Although the smaller RAF fighter planes were able to take off and set down together in groups, the huge B-24s would have to land one at a time. Without landing gear, the Texas Buckaroo would have to belly in. Due to the danger of a fiery crash, she would come in last.

The first B-24 cleared to land was the Sledge Hammer. Those gathered on the ground were amazed that the American plane, battered by German fighters, was even capable of flying. One of the two vertical tails was missing, and the left engine's propeller was bent so far back that it had lodged into the wing. Struggling with the controls, the exhausted pilot lowered the bomber close to the field and cut the remaining engines

early. The plane silently dropped the last few
feet, until its wheels hit the ground with a heavy
thud. Powerless, the Sledge Hammer rolled to a
quiet stop at the far end of the field.

Then the Tall Order approached the field.
Although the plane looked relatively undamaged,
there was definitely something wrong. Once the
Tall Order came closer to the field, the problem
became apparent. Gaping bullet holes riddled the
plane. Huge pieces of the tail and wing flaps had
been shot off, making them useless. The pilot
controlled the bomber by throttling the engines

up and down to direct their approach and correct for wind changes. Captain Dawson could see both the pilot and co-pilot feverishly handling the controls of the lurching B-24 as it neared the ground.

Finally, its wheels slammed into the turf. After bouncing off the runway several times, the pilot of the Tall Order was able to maneuver his plane behind the hardstand. Now the field was clear for the last damaged B-24.

Trailing thick black smoke, the Texas Buckaroo turned to approach the airfield for landing. While waiting for the other airplanes to clear out of his way, Captain Ross had maneuvered so he could land on the far side. If the "Buckaroo" were to crash there, it wouldn't damage the fighter squadron's airstrip or any other planes. In his mind, Captain Ross felt it was the least he could do for his new RAF friends, especially since they were the ones who helped get him and his crew this far.

Down on the ground, Dawson, Harry, and the rest silently watched the Texas Buckaroo straighten for the approach and then begin its risky descent. Captain Ross skillfully piloted his plane to within a few feet of the turf. Without landing gear to cushion the impact, he struggled with the controls to inch even lower and still maintain a level flight.

Inside the Buckaroo, Ross shouted to his crew, "Okay, boys, this is it! Everyone get in your crash positions!"

Then he cut the remaining engines. For a moment, the people on the ground and in the plane held their breath.

An instant later, metal met ground. To those watching, it looked as though the Texas Buckaroo gently settled to the earth, sliding easily along the grass to a stop at the end of the field. But to the men huddled inside, the sound of the 30 ton airplane grinding through the dirt was deafening. The crippled bomber violently shook, while pieces of sod and rocks flew past the windows. For the weary crew, the last nine hundred feet of the mission was the most terrifying. With one final lurch and a slight twist, the flight of the Texas Buckaroo came to an end.

A relieved Captain Ross took a deep breath. Looking at his co-pilot he started in a practiced voice, "Shut down procedure!"

"Chief," the co-pilot interrupted, "there's nothing left to shut down."

Captain Ross looked around the battered cockpit and then reached over to pat his co-pilot's back.

With a big grin, Ross unbuckled his seat straps and shouted to his crew, "All righty boys, let's call it a day and get out of here!"

Captain Ross and his crew climbed from the hulk of their broken B-24. Shaken, but alive, they pounded each other on the back with hearty praise.

Sirens screaming, the airstrip fire truck and ambulance tore across the field to the disabled airplane. Immediately, almost every pilot, mechanic, and crewman at the airfield, as well as Harry Winslow, had rushed over to the Texas Buckaroo.

Captains Dawson and Simms reached out to shake hands and congratulate their new American friends. Then the pair of RAF pilots escorted the Americans back to the Operations Building to meet Colonel Harrison.

CHAPTER TWELVE

MISSION COMPLETE

With everyone gathered together in the briefing room, Colonel Harrison was able to confirm to all the exhausted fliers that their mission was a complete success. They had badly damaged the supply lines to the coastal fortifications by demolishing both the bridge and railway yard. And more importantly, the destruction of the oil depot would significantly cut back on the fuel supply used for German air raids on England.

"Unfortunately, my mechanics have just informed me that the B-24s you landed here have been determined unrepairable. All three are considered lost and will have to be scrapped," Colonel Harrison told Captain Ross.

Ross nodded his head at the unfortunate news and replied, "Three planes lost all right, but without yer boys up there today, Colonel, none of us would'a come home alive. With your permission, we'd like to put on a little 'git-together' for you and yer squadron to say thank you."

Colonel Harrison looked at Captain Dawson and the other RAF pilots and asked, "Will you men help Captain Ross with everything he needs?"

"Yes sir!" Dawson snapped with a crisp salute.

"Well then," Harrison replied to Captain Ross, "everything would seem to be in order. But, right now I need to finish the mission notes with my pilots. Why don't you take a few minutes to get familiar with Hampton Airfield."

Captain Ross saluted Colonel Harrison and left the room so the RAF pilots could finish their meeting. Stepping outside, Ross noticed young Harry Winslow sitting in the grassy yard in front of the Operations Building.

"Howdy there, young man!" Ross greeted Harry with a smile. Extending his hand, he introduced himself.

"Captain Sam Ross, United States Army Air Force. What's yer name, son?"

Having never heard an actual southern accent before,

Harry was a bit startled by the boisterous American pilot. Jumping to his feet, Harry reached to shake the outstretched hand of Captain Ross.

"My name is Harry Winslow, sir."

"So you're the Winslow boy. Glad to meet ya!"

"How do you know me?" Harry sheepishly asked.

"I'll tell ya, kid," Ross replied, "It was a long ride home for me and my boys. Captain Dawson and I had plenty of time to talk about lots of things."

Surprised that he would be a topic of conversation among the pilots, Harry couldn't help but ask, "What did he tell you?"

Ross started in his heavy accent, "Dawson mentioned somethin' about you always bein' here to see him and his boys off on their missions. And then watchin' for 'em to come back again."

Wondering aloud he continued, "What else did he say? Oh yeah, he said you know more about their flights than Colonel Harrison does. And he also pointed out that you're the only member of the squadron who has his own bedroom!"

"A member of the squadron?" Harry thought. Harry smiled at the idea of Captain Dawson considering him a member of the squadron. But

the warm moment faded
when he thought of his
mishap with Mr. Reid's shed.

Ashamed, Harry
admitted to Ross, "But, I'm
not brave enough to be one
of them."

"Brave?" Ross barked. "I'm tellin' ya kid,
bravery is all well and good, but being responsible,
now that's the makin' of a good man in my book!"

Harry was surprised at the American's
statement. In his young mind he always thought
the key to his fighter pilot friends was being brave
and strong.

Unconvinced, Harry said, "You've got to be
brave to face those German fighters."

"That's true, boy," Ross replied nodding his
head. "But it's responsibility that keeps us
climbing back into the cockpit everyday. It was
Captain Dawson's sense of responsibility that made
him stick with me and my boys when the chips
were down. A brave man can always get himself
out of a jam. But a responsible man, he's the one
who can get everybody out!"

Ross stopped for a moment and then finished,

"I'm tellin' ya kid, be responsible and face things
head on...the rest will come."

Harry looked at Captain Ross, speechless.
So absorbed in everything Ross had said, all
Harry could do was nod. Ross smiled and patted
the twelve year old on his shoulder.

"These men are lucky to have you, Harry."

Then the American pilot began to walk away.
Turning back, Ross called to Harry, "Hey kid,
we're having a big party tonight. Y'all make sure
you come now, ya' hear?"

Harry nodded his head in amazement, an
ear to ear grin stretching across his face.
Watching Ross stroll out to the airfield, Harry
barely noticed Captain Dawson coming down the
steps of the Operations Building.

"Harry," Captain Dawson shouted to the
Winslow boy. "Did you want to talk to me earlier, lad?"

With the words of Captain Ross still ringing
in his head, Harry called back, "Yes sir, I did...
but...well, not anymore."

Scrambling across the field he shouted, "I
need to go, Captain, I have to take care of something important!"

CHAPTER THIRTEEN

BEING RESPONSIBLE

Harry realized he and his friends needed to take responsibility for the accident with Mr. Reid's shed, regardless of their fears. He felt if they fixed the shed, they could make things right with Mr. Reid. It was the trustworthy thing to do.

Harry ran to gather Stuart and Erin together so he could explain his idea to them. They agreed it was what they should do, and hoped that the rest would work out for the best.

However, "Mad Man" Reid was known as the meanest man in the county, and Harry worried about his reaction to their solution. On the way to Mr. Reid's house, they talked in whispers while framing up a plan that would make things right again.

Stepping onto the stoop of Mr. Reid's house, Harry, Stuart and Erin knocked quickly on the front door. They anxiously waited for someone to answer. Finally, the knob slowly turned and the door began to creak open on its rusty hinges. The three children held their breath in anticipation.

"Who's there?" asked a cranky voice.

"It's me, Mr. Reid," began Harry, in as brave a voice as he could muster. "Harry Winslow...and my two friends, Stuart and Erin."

The door opened the rest of the way. Stepping out of the shadows and into the light, Mr. Reid moved closer to examine the three frightened youngsters. A frown clouded his face when he recognized them as the ones responsible for knocking down his chicken coop.

"What do you little hooligans want? Haven't I already seen enough of you for one day?"

Harry shrank back as Mr. Reid continued to crowd them.

"Mr. Reid," Harry politely continued, "I know we caused you quite a bit of trouble today, but if you'll let me explain..."

"Explain what, young man? That you smashed my shed and scattered my chickens to the winds? Is that what you want to explain?" Mr. Reid sternly asked.

Harry swallowed hard, "I was just trying to get my kite off your chicken coop and it broke underneath me."

Mr. Reid glared at Harry, "Look, I spent most of the day collecting my chickens! Now I have a shed to repair before nightfall, and I suppose you want your kites back!"

Harry and the other two shivered, fearful of being scolded by the old man and then punished by their parents.

Anticipating the worst, Harry began stammering, "I'm very sorry. I didn't mean for it to collapse like that. I was trying to get my kite. I hope I didn't hurt any of your chickens. I... I..."

Holding up his hand to stop Harry's apologetic rambling, Mr. Reid barked, "The worst part was that all the while I was rounding up the chickens, I was worried that some young boy may have been hurt!"

Mr. Reid and Harry looked at each other for a long moment. Neither side said anything.

Then Mr. Reid demanded, "Just what do you want from me?"

"Sir," Harry bravely replied, "we brought some tools and extra wood and shingles in order to fix your shed. If that would be acceptable to you, we would like to start now."

Mr. Reid eyed the children standing on his porch. Crossing his arms over his chest, he looked over at the broken shed.

"Well, you broke it. I guess it's your responsibility to fix it."

Harry turned to Stuart and Erin. They agreed it was their responsibility. All they wanted was a chance to make things right.

Mr. Reid nodded his head and pointed at the wrecked chicken coop, "Go then...fix it!"

The children sprang from the porch and ran to the demolished shed. They walked around and examined the condition of the coop. In order to start the needed repairs, they had to clear out all of the broken bits of rotten wood from the heap.

After a few minutes of picking up the splintered pieces, Stuart shouted for Harry.

"Look what I found!" he called, while pulling

something from the pile of wood. "Our kites are here, and they're still in one piece! Mine just needs a little repair and yours looks to be in pretty good shape."

Stuart handed them to Harry. The two boys examined the kites and were happy to see them in such good condition.

After tossing a chunk of broken wood aside, Erin pointed out to Harry, "Now instead of making a whole new kite, you can just find someone to paint a picture of a Hawker Hurricane on it."

Over on the other side of the shed, Mr. Reid was silently supervising the children's work. Listening intently to their conversation, he came around the corner toward them.

"Why don't I just hold on to those for a while?" he barked.

Fearing he would never see the kites again, Harry reluctantly handed them over to a stern Mr. Reid. Snatching them out of Harry's hands, Mr. Reid turned on his heel and headed back to his house.

Over his shoulder he directed, "Now be sure to build carefully! I have chickens that need a safe place by nightfall!"

After a couple hours of hard work, the shed was rebuilt. The two boys used fresh wood planks to replace the rotted ones that had buckled under Harry earlier in the day. Carefully, Erin nailed on shingles to keep out the rain. Then Harry shaved the door and oiled the hinges so it would swing freely.

By this time, Mr. Reid was rocking on his front porch and supervising from a distance. Seeing they had finished, Mr. Reid motioned them back to his weathered house.

When Harry, Stuart and Erin reached the porch he asked, "Do your parents know about this little mishap?"

Sheepishly the youngsters looked at each other. The expression on Erin's face did little to hide her fear about being punished.

Harry hesitantly replied, "No, they don't. At least not yet, anyway."

"Good," replied Mr. Reid, while reaching out to shake their hands. "I believe you don't need to worry them about this."

The children quietly nodded their heads. Although greatly relieved, they were even more surprised that the man they had thought of as

"Mad Man" Reid, had so kindly offered to keep them out of trouble.

Then, Mr. Reid surprised them once more. Reaching behind the graying front door, he pulled out two kites and handed them to the boys.

They were glad to have their kites back. Stuart immediately began to inspect his and noticed Mr. Reid had replaced the tattered paper with a fresh, crisp sheet. His kite looked as new as Harry's.

Even better, when both boys turned their kites over to look at the front, they could hardly contain their excitement. Skillfully painted on each kite was a picture of an RAF Hawker Hurricane diving from the clouds!

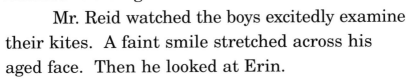

Mr. Reid watched the boys excitedly examine their kites. A faint smile stretched across his aged face. Then he looked at Erin.

Reaching back behind the door once more Mr. Reid said, "I have one for you too, young lady."

Erin stepped forward and reached for her new kite.

"Thank you! Did you paint a picture of a

Hurricane on mine?" she eagerly asked.

"Why no, I didn't." Mr. Reid replied. "I feel a lady should have something a little more refined. Something more graceful."

Happy to simply receive her own kite, Erin worked to hide her disappointment that Mr. Reid hadn't painted hers with a Hurricane like Harry's. But when she turned the kite over, an ear to ear grin raced across her face and she let out a shout that startled the two boys.

"Mr. Reid," Erin exclaimed, "it's beautiful!"

"What is it, Erin?" Stuart asked, trying to see the picture.

Harry turned to look at Erin's kite. In contrast to the rugged Hurricanes Mr. Reid had painted on the boys' kites, Erin's was adorned with the sleek lines and graceful wings of a Spitfire.

"It's a Spitfire!" Harry shouted. "Look, Stuart. Mr. Reid painted an RAF Spitfire fighter plane on Erin's kite!"

Stuart looked at the kite and then at Erin. With just a slight nod of his head, Erin's older brother let her know just how special her kite was.

Then Mr. Reid motioned for Harry, Stuart and Erin to gather close. "Listen to me, youngsters," he said. "The only thing around here older than me was that shed. Thank you for repairing it."

The children, dirty from repairing the shed, stared at each other. They were astonished at just how wrong they were about "Mad Man" Reid.

"Thank you so very much, Mr. Reid," Harry said. "These kites are..."

"Glorious," finished Erin.

"Well, I look forward to seeing your planes flying in the sky tomorrow," replied Mr. Reid pointing at the kites. "But I would suggest staying away from the chicken coop. Those chickens can't handle so much excitement!"

"Yes, sir!" all three replied in unison.

With the shed fixed and their problem resolved, the children started for home. Along the way, Harry, Stuart and Erin chatted about the day's events. They talked about their new friend, Mr. Reid, and how they would like to go back and get to know him better. They talked about being responsible and doing the right thing.   But most of all, they laughed about how silly Harry looked falling through the shed.

When they reached the Winslow home, Harry bounded for the front porch.

Before Harry opened the screen door, Stuart called out, "Thanks for getting us out of the jam, Harry!"

Harry waved back to his friends, Stuart and Erin. Remembering everything Captain Ross had  told him, Harry looked at his kite for a moment. "He was right," Harry thought. "Be responsible and the rest will come."

CHAPTER FOURTEEN

FAREWELL TO THE TEXAS BUCKAROO

Late that afternoon, everyone at Hampton Airfield made their way to a campfire burning not far from the crippled Texas Buckaroo. Finished with the repairs to Mr. Reid's shed, Harry Winslow also joined the men who had gathered on the field.

The pilots of the 14th Squadron had helped Captain Ross and his crew put together a real Texas style barbecue. Smoke and steam billowed up from pots of food cooking over  the fire. Talking to the base cook, Captain Ross detailed the specifics of how to make, what he called, the "perfect" barbecue sauce. Once the cook seemed to understand his recipe, Ross stepped away from the makeshift kitchen and joined Captain Dawson under the wing of the Texas Buckaroo.

"This is indeed a fine banquet you've put on," Dawson told Captain Ross.

"I'm glad y'all appreciate a good picnic 'round here," Ross replied.

Captain Dawson continued, "I'll drive you and your crew back to Manchester tomorrow morning. But for tonight, Simms and I have put up a bunk for you in our quarters."

The American pilot turned and brushed his hand over the picture of the bucking bronco painted on the nose of his plane.

"Thank you, Dawson," Captain Ross said. "But if it's all the same to you, I think I'll just stay out here with the old 'Buckaroo' tonight."

A bit puzzled, Dawson replied, "Certainly Sam, if that's what you want."

Captain Ross stepped over to where the emblems of the bombs were painted under the pilot's window.

"She's headed for the scrap yard this time, for sure," Ross said with some sadness in his voice. Reaching up he patted the bottom of the wing and continued, "After the party, I think I'll just bed down right here under her wing."

82

A fellow flyer, Dawson understood his new friend's feelings about the loss of his airplane. After a brief silence, he made a suggestion designed to cheer up the American.

"It's still early, Sam. Let's enjoy a bit of that feast and then you can tell me about some of your other missions in the Texas Buckaroo."

Ross turned from the plane to look at Dawson. A huge smile broke across his face.

Then he hollered, "Whoooey! There's sure some stories to tell!"

The two pilots rejoined the rest of the men hovering about the barbecue. Harry Winslow was delighted to be surrounded by Dawson, Ross and all the other pilots. For the rest of the evening he enjoyed the accent of the American fliers and their heroic tales.

Captain Ross was in his glory recounting the missions of the Texas Buckaroo and her crew. With everyone huddled around the glowing embers of the fire, he shared his stories of adventure far into the night.

Exhausted, Harry's head soon fell limp onto Dawson's shoulder. The combination of the hard work repairing Mr. Reid's shed and the late hour

"Excuse me gentlemen," Dawson said... "But I'm responsible for getting Harry home."

had finally caught up with him.

"Excuse me, gentlemen," Dawson said to the others. "But I'm responsible for getting Harry home."

Captain Dawson scooped the sleeping boy into his arms and carried him across the dark airfield. Bright stars twinkling from above seemed to smile down on the merry group. Slipping through the hedgerow fence, he followed the worn, dirt path back to the Winslow home. Before Dawson finished climbing the steps to the porch, Mrs. Winslow was there to meet him.

"Thank you for bringing Harry home, Captain," Mrs. Winslow called to Dawson as he approached the front door of the two story farm house.

"I'll take him up to his bedroom, if you like," Dawson suggested.

Mrs. Winslow nodded her agreement.

 Dawson carefully climbed the stairs to Harry's bedroom. Gently, he laid the sleeping boy on his bed. Stepping back, Dawson noticed Harry's kite hanging on the wall. Even in the dim light, Mr. Reid's

painting of the fighter plane was remarkable.
Dawson couldn't help but smile when he noticed
the squadron markings painted onto the plane.
Harry had slightly changed Mr. Reid's picture by
adding in the letters HP and A along the body.
They were the identification marks of Dawson's
Hawker Hurricane.

On his way back to Hampton, Dawson could
hear the southern accent of Captain Ross echoing
across the airfield. Mixed with laughter from the
other pilots, Ross and Simms were still telling
stories when Dawson returned. Settling in with
his friends, he joined the other men spinning
their tales well into the early morning hours. In the
end, the three pilots Ross, Dawson, and Simms
were too tired to return to their quarters. Together,
they all spent the night under the protective wing
of the Texas Buckaroo.

IN HINDSIGHT

By the end of 1940, the Battle of Britain had been won by the pilots and crews of the Royal Air Force. However, the German Luftwaffe continued massive night bombing raids on London until the spring of 1941. During this period, known as "The Blitz", London was bombed practically every night in an attempt to disrupt manufacturing and terrify the English population. In addition to the constant bombing, German ships and submarines maintained a blockade designed to cut off the delivery of necessary food and supplies to England. In response to these tactics, Britain fought back with bombs.

The Bomber Command branch of the RAF had been developed for just this task. While RAF Fighter Command defended Britain from German air raids, Bomber Command was used to launch a counterattack. When the threat of German invasion reached its peak, RAF bombers flew mission after mission to attack the German forces assembling in French coastal cities. After the invasion was canceled, Bomber Command redirected their missions to targets in occupied Europe and Germany.

Daytime bombing missions provided the most accurate results, but also suffered the highest losses of planes and

men. Even though the large bombers were heavily armed
with machine guns and flew in large groups for protection,
they suffered severe punishment from the fast moving
German fighter planes. Quickly, the RAF learned to team
their bombers with squadrons of fighter planes in order to
shield them from attack by enemy fighters. Unfortunately,
many bombing missions were required to fly to targets
beyond the limited range of the RAF fighter escorts.
Losses from these long-range missions were so severe that
the RAF changed tactics and used the cover of darkness
for protection, eventually converting to night bombing
exclusively.

America entered the war in late 1941 and joined the
British in their fight against Germany. By spring of 1942,
swarms of American planes and pilots united with the RAF
as allies in the battle against the Luftwaffe.

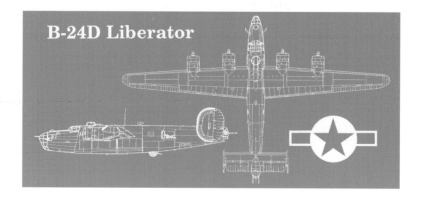

B-24D Liberator

Allied (British and American) commanders agreed that bombing of German military, transportation, and manufacturing targets was essential to winning the war. However, they strongly disagreed over tactics. The Americans favored daytime precision bombing. The British, having already suffered the setbacks of daylight bombing missions, argued that night bombing was more prudent. The issue was resolved when the Allies agreed to an around-the-clock bombing campaign designed to dismantle German weapons production and win back air superiority over the European mainland. Royal Air Force Bomber Command would bomb by night and the Americans by day.

Fighter planes were used to escort the American B-17 and B-24 heavy bombers on missions into enemy territory. Called "Little Friends" by the bomber crews, Allied escorts would intercept any German fighter planes encountered in route to their targets. Short and medium range bombing missions to Belgium or France enjoyed the protection of their Little Friends for the entire mission. But the limited range of English Hurricanes and Spitfires, as well as the American P-47 Thunderbolt, forced them to leave the bomber formations on their own when the mission traveled deep into German territory. The Luftwaffe learned to simply wait until the fighter support had turned back and then launched squadrons of German planes to cut the bombers down.

By October of 1943, American daylight bombing missions into Germany resulted in catastrophic losses. Between enemy fighters and flak (shells that explode metal fragments into the air), as much as fifty percent of the planes sent on some missions never returned. In response, the Allies suspended long-range daylight bombing operations.

American B-24s attack a German oil refinery in Ploesti, Rumania.

The development of long-range fighters such as the P-51 and the use of drop tanks containing reserve fuel to extend the range of other fighter planes provided the means to reduce the staggering bomber losses. With these improvements, bomber crews could depend on fighter protection to and from targets deep in enemy territory. The combination of new long-range fighters with daylight bombing accuracy attained remarkable results.

By April of 1944, the new fighters had won air superiority over western Europe and Germany. Allied bombing had shattered German weapons manufacturing, transportation, and fuel supplies. Protected by their Little Friends, Allied bomber crews faced fewer and fewer enemy fighters. Hundreds of planes and thousands of lives were saved by fighter pilots escorting the huge bombers all the way to their targets and bringing them back home again safely.

Allied fighter planes, known as "Little Friends" to bomber crews, assemble above.

GLOSSARY

Allies: The combination of American, British, and Russian military forces.

Aviators: Pilots or airmen.

B-24 Liberator: An American long-range heavy bomber protected by machine gun placements in the waist, tail, top, bottom and nose. Liberators had a 106 foot wingspan, four engines and carried a crew of ten men.

Bombardier: The crew member responsible for targeting and dropping of bombs.

Captain: A military officer ranking below colonel and above lieutenant.

Colonel: A military officer ranking below general and above captain.

Fuselage: The central body of an airplane.

Hardstand: A hard surfaced area next to an airstrip used for parking planes and ground vehicles.

Hawker Hurricane: A type of British fighter plane.

Hedgerow: A row of bushes or small trees that form a fence.

Intercept: To stop or interrupt the progress of enemy aircraft.

Lieutenant: A military officer ranking below captain.

Messerschmitt 109: A type of German fighter plane (also Me 109).

Operations Building: The airfield's central administration building.

Petrol: British term for gasoline.

Rally Point: Location where numerous squadrons would assemble creating a large formation.

Stick or Yoke: The control stick of an airplane used for steering.

Yanks: Nickname for Americans.